Everything Happens for a Reason

JESSICA STEVENS

DEDICATION

To Mr. Dodd, and everyone else who made
this dream become a reality.

CHAPTER ONE

One Saturday morning in March, the sun was shining, and the sky was a beautiful light blue. It was a warm spring day. Emily was walking down the road to her grandma's house. She was listening to tunes on her mobile and enjoying the heat from the sun's rays. She loved music. It was her favourite lesson at school, and she was the best singer in her year.

Emily was wearing a shoulder-less white top and lace white shorts. She was carrying a small white shoulder bag and her hair was in perfect curls, blowing gently in the cool breeze.

She looked up from her phone to see a boy staring at her.

He had a gentle smile and rosy cheeks. He was holding a sparkly lead; on the end was a white fluffy Pomeranian waddling proudly. The dog was called Rex and looked like a tiny fluffy cloud. His dog was her dream pet. He was a new boy who had just moved in down the road. She smiled back at him.

On the inside, they were both blushing. Her grandma came out of her house and gave her a hug and noticed she was staring back at the boy. Gran turned around to see the boy enter his house,

"Not bad," she said, now Emily's blush was evident on the outside. She smiled at the old lady and they both went into her house.

The boy was called Matthew, Matt to his friends. Little did they know that they would become inseparable. Little did he know that she didn't have the best life. Little did they know that everything would go horribly wrong for them… in the end.

The following Monday, Matt went to the local school, which was a thirty-minute walk away. He didn't know that the mysterious girl was going to be at that school. He was a stranger to the school. All he was given was a girl's name on a scrap piece of paper; a girl who would show him around and make him feel welcome.

He walked all over the school trying to find the music room. Music was his favourite lesson, so he was happy as well as nervous. He knocked on the door, took a deep breath and walked in. The teacher was sat by the piano and

Emily was standing next to it. She was totally focused on singing. She had the voice of an angel and was unlike anything he had heard before. He was mesmerized. A girl sat on the chair nearby. Other students focused in smaller groups. She didn't notice he was there. Once finished, they both walked away. He stared at her until she had disappeared. He walked up to the teacher and reluctantly handed over the ripped piece of paper. The teacher read the name and called Emily in. It was the girl with the amazing voice, the same girl from the dog walk!

At the time he thought she was beautiful, and her voice echoed repetitively in my mind. It sounded like Heaven. When he found out it was her, he was spellbound. He would have the opportunity to talk to this girl who he had not been able to stop thinking about. He suddenly felt less nervous and more excited. Excited for the future. On looking into her deep blue shimmering eyes again, he was hypnotised. He had a weird and wonderful feeling about seeing her again, how could he ever forget that face. He was pleased to know that he could see her every day. Moving here was good after all.

Emily was distracted when he came into her lesson. She couldn't concentrate and tried her best to hide it. She just wanted the song to be over. When it did finish, she panicked. She didn't know what to do. She just left... left as quickly as she could. She knew that she recognised him and that had seen him before. She couldn't forget that face; the New Boy. She couldn't stop thinking about him. It was a feeling which she had never experienced before. She just wanted to get to know him, everything about him. She already felt like they could be really good friends. It made Emily really happy to know that she was the one chosen to show him around. Maybe he would be the person to make her life better again. She could only hope and dream. After the lesson Katie said knowingly,

"I saw the way he looked at you… and I saw the way you looked at him"

Two months passed and Emily and Matt had spent a lot of time together. Emily had made Matt feel very welcome, in the area and in school. Their relationship grew stronger and pretty soon, they began spending all day, every day together.

Emily and Katie were sitting at the back of the class, Matt was at the front. The teacher put a video on the screen. Emily was staring at Matt. Katie looked at Emily.

"You like him, don't you?" Katie whispered.

"I don't like him," she replied

"I think I love him." She muttered under her breath. Katie smirked.

"I knew it!" she shouted.

"Shhh" Emily said desperately.

"Don't tell him," she pleaded. Katie smiled. "Don't!"

"Okay, okay I won't… yet." After class Emily bought lunch. Matt and Katie were waiting for her. Katie noticed Matt looking at Emily.

"You like her, don't you?"

"No… I think I love her"

"I knew it" Katie said excitedly, her plan was to get them together.

"Please don't tell her"

"Okay." There was an awkward silence.

"There's something you need to know about Emily" Katie said.

"What? Is she okay?" Matt said worriedly.

"She's okay. At least, that's what she tells us."

"I don't understand, what are you talking about?"

"Don't worry; she can tell you herself… just don't tell her what I told you… Hey Emily!" They walked away and Matt followed on.

A few days later, Emily was late for school. Only fifteen minutes but it was long enough for Matt to realise something was wrong. He was waiting impatiently for her at music. He knew something was wrong. She came rushing in.

"I'm so sorry I'm late" she took a breath and walked into the small room where Matt was.

"Em, hey are you okay? What's happened?"

She threw her bag on the floor, fell back on her chair and covered her face. She had been crying and was too ashamed to show him. He grabbed her arm and pulled it away. He saw her tears. "Tell me what's up."

"I'm tired" she replied. He knew she was lying because she wouldn't look him in the eye. He also sat down.

"Go on tell me," he said reassuringly. She slowly lifted her head to look at him. She saw in his eyes he wanted to help. She knew she could trust him enough to tell him her deepest, darkest secret. She was ashamed to show him. She never cried especially not in front of anyone.

"It's-it's my grandma. She... she's dying. She can't die, she can't."

"At least you've got your parents support,"

"That's what I'm afraid of. I don't have their support. I never have." She admitted.

"What are you talking about?"

"Well, at the age of ten I came home from school one day. I found my dad asleep on the sofa. I tried to wake him up. He didn't wake up. I shouted and screamed."

"What happened" he asked.

"He didn't wake up." There was a long pause. "The only thing I could do was ring an ambulance. They came and took us both to the hospital."

"Where was your mum?"

"They were out shopping. They had no idea." He couldn't look at her.

"I sat by his bed. His eyes began to shut, and he grabbed my hand. I remember like it was yesterday. He whispered, 'my beautiful princess, I love you so much and even though I will not be there I will always be with you and I know you are going to make me so proud."

"I'm so sorry Em," Matt said trying to cheer her up.

"He held my face with tears in his eyes." She continued.

"I didn't know what was happening. We had a thing where we would always say when we said goodbye. It means we would always love each other. He slowly began to close his eyes. I said to him, 'Dad, I love you, always...' and then his hand went cold on mine. The computer made a continuous ringing sound that still haunts me to this day." Matt moved closer to her. He wanted to comfort her, but he didn't know how to.

"I was dragged out of the room. I was locked out. I watched by the open window. One of the nurses closed the blind. The nurse came out of the room, she said, 'Sorry sweetie' and walked away." Matt had tears in his eyes to.

"All I remember is falling to the floor and crying. Five years ago, and I still blame myself. If only I came home from school earlier, if I had rung an ambulance sooner or told the nurse as soon as he woke up."

"It's not your fault. Don't say that." He said a little too loudly.

"Now I feel the pain. Losing him was so hard. Every day is a battle. Eventually Mum and Grandma turned up. They saw me on the floor. They had kept a secret from me. He was dying of cancer and they never told me. I will never forgive them for that. Never." There was a pause again.

"When we went home it was so weird… without him. Everyone told me that it would get better over time. It never did. At the worst time of my life I needed her. Her love. Her comfort. I never got it."

"What do you mean?" he pleaded.

"She would always stumble to the shops and waste our money on alcohol. Then come home and drink herself unconscious. She got addicted. Every day I had to fend for myself. Grieving and desperate. But left by myself. I was the only person at Dad's funeral. Grandma was too ill to come. Even though she wanted to. I visit him every day after school. To make my life even worse she met someone. Neil. He makes me feel sick."

"Why?" he wanted to know more but didn't want to sound rude.

"He brainwashed her into thinking she can't live without him. He isn't a nice man. He goes out every week. Cheat and get drunk but when Mum did, he would get so angry. He hits Mum if he feels like it. If he is incredibly angry, he hits me too. He does unspeakable things to all women. He repulses me. It is acceptable for him to do anything but when a woman does it, she's out or order." Emily spat as she said this. "I'm terrified, in fear of my life every time I go near him. I don't know what he's capable of."

"I will protect you; I promise." He said. His hand moving closer to hers.

"Now what am I going to do. I have no one left to rely on. I can't go back. I can't."

Matt looked horrified. He couldn't believe that one perfect girl could have such a terrible life. He couldn't believe it; but never for one second did he believe that she could be lying.

"Oh, Em, that's horrible. Why didn't you tell me before?"

"I just didn't want you to treat me differently. That's why no one knows. Not even the teachers. Just Katie. Please don't tell anyone."

Emily stood up in pain. Her whole world, which she had left, was crumbling in front of her. Matt stood up as well. He held her hand to calm her down. She was shaking. He could see the desperation in her eyes. A tear fell down her cheek. He held her face. He wanted her to know that he's there for her. Their faces slowly got closer. Their lips touched. For a minute everything went silent. It comforted her but she got scared. She didn't know he liked her. Emily realised what had just happened. She was scared that her feelings would ruin their friendship. He meant so much to her, she couldn't lose another person she trusted. She grabbed her bag and coat and ran out of the room.

"I-I can't do this."

"Em, Emily wait," he ran after her, but she was too quick. The lesson had ended, and it was break. It gave her a chance to run.

"Emily, you don't understand" he shouted after her. But it was too late, she was gone.

"I love you," he whispered. She was hiding around the corner. She heard him. She felt the same but was wary because of George. He was her ex. George had cheated on her and she had never trusted anyone in the same way again. He was jealous at anyone who looked at her other than a friend. He hated Matt. He was in the classroom where this happened but at a distance. He saw what had happened and hated that fact that she had moved on and hated him.

Outside Katie was waiting. As Emily rushed out of the door she shouted,

"Hey, Em what's the rush?"

"I'll explain later, but if you see Matt, you never saw me." She knew that they would never argue or say anything mean. Katie was really confused why she didn't want him to know where she was.

"Something happened in there and I'm scared." Emily said running and hiding behind the wall. Matt followed seconds later. He shouts her name, but she just hid. Katie was witnessing the situation in total confusion.

"Emily wait, you don't understand. I love you and I want you." He desperately shouted. She slowly appeared from the wall.

"Do-do you mean that?"

"Yes," he grabbed her hand.

"I love you more than you could ever know. I want to care for you, support you through the rest of our lives. Will you love me too?"

Katie smirked. Emily smiled like she was the happiest girl in the world. She hugged him and he hugged her back. Nothing could spoil their moment.

A fortnight later Emily's grandma had died. She went around her house and found her dead. Once again, she felt the loss and once again, she was the only one at a funeral. Her life crumbled more. There was hardly anything left to fall. She was alone, nowhere to go, no one to talk to. Matt was ringing her all day. She would always answer her phone but not that day. He was getting very worried. He thought he could find her in the graveyard, but she wasn't in the usual spot. Standing by a fresh, newly placed grave. He was confused but had a flashback of his happiest memory and remembered that her gran was dying.

"Emily," he said softly. She looked up, her eyes sore and red.

"I went around her house and found her asleep in her bed only she wasn't asleep. I lay by her side until I could move. What else is going to go wrong?"

She fell to her knees in tears. He sat on the floor and held her. Held her tight, show her he was there for her. After a while Matt's phone rang it was his mum. She told him to come home. He wanted Emily to live with him. So, he could give her the support she never had.

"Please Mum, let her move in, she needs me. And she can have Hannah's old room. Mum, please we both need this." His mum knew that she needed him and allowed her to move in.

Emily's happiness was reunited with her after some time, enhanced by Matt arranging a special surprise for her. She was out with friends one day and he planted a tree in memory of her grandma. She was so happy and grateful for everything he sacrificed for her. Soon the tree flowered, and it stood gracefully, towering for everyone to see in the park. She needed all the help she could get, even though she wouldn't admit it. Now, she was part of the family. They had a few weeks of happiness where they thought nothing could go wrong. Until…

Emily was getting ready for school one day. She was brushing her hair and she noticed something. Something on her leg. It was a dark spot like smudged ink. She was slightly worried but didn't really think about it. There was a knock on the door, it was Matt.

"Hey, are you okay?" she quickly crossed her leg to hide the mark. He worried about her too much, the slightest little thing he would worry about.

"Yeah, I'm coming down now." She put her hairbrush on the table and followed him down the stairs. She went into the kitchen with Matt's mum. She bent down to get a drink and

Matt's mum noticed the mark on her leg. She got anxious very quickly.

"I'll take you there." she said.

"Where?" Emily asked, very confused.

"Hospital," she whispered.

"What? Why?" Emily became even more confused.

"For the mark on your leg. We need a doctor's opinion." She continued softly.

"Matt! You go to school and Emily will follow you."

"Okay, see you later." Matt said, waving goodbye as he passed the kitchen. Unaware of what's about to come. He walked out of the door and went to school. His mum waited until he was out of sight, grabbed her hand and pulled her to the car. They drove to the hospital.

Emily was panicking. She felt even worse when she got to the school later.

"I can't tell him. It will crush him." Even though she was suffering she put everyone's needs before hers.

"Don't worry about him. Trust me, he will live, but if you don't stop stressing you probably won't. He will be okay. Just tell him carefully."

"Of course, I will, I just don't want to hurt him."

"I promise you everything will be okay. Everything happens for a reason." Emily took a breath and exited the car. She slowly walked up to the school.

Meanwhile, at school Matt was worrying enormously, as usual. "Where is she?" he asked Katie, pacing the corridor.

"She's never been this late."

"She's okay she'll be here in a minute... Look here she is."

Matt ran up to her and held her tightly. "Where have you been? I was so worried." He stepped back and held her face.

"Are you okay?"

"Yeah, I'm fine."

"Okay, good." He believed everything she said, but Katie saw straight through the lies.

"What really happened?" Katie asked, crossing her arms.

"Shhh… be quiet. I'll tell you, follow me." She held her arm and dragged her to the toilet block. Matt came back and they had disappeared. He was relieved that she was back in school but was puzzled when they had disappeared.

In the toilet block there were boys' toilets on one side and girls' on the other side, with the sinks in between. Emily was standing with her back to the door and Katie was in front of the mirror.

"What really happened?" Katie asked, staring at her intently.

"Well, there was something on my leg and Matt's mum took me to the hospital…" Emily's eyes filled with tears.

Matt walked into the toilet block and hid behind the lockers.

"T-they said it was the early stages of melanoma, a type of skin cancer. I have to leave school and recover... and I'm so, so scared." Katie hugged her. "Don't worry, I almost have a hundred percent chance of survival."

Matt, in his hiding place, could not believe what he was hearing.

"You have to tell him, and soon!"

Matt tripped over and in a manic attempt to save himself reached out to grab something and crashed against the locker. The girls turned around to see him staring at her in disbelief.

"How much of that did you hear?" Emily asked in horror.

"Enough."

"I... I'm so...sorry. I... I didn't want you to find out like this." He took a step forward and held his hands out, Emily took them and squeezed tight,

"Don't worry about me. Everything will be alright." She swallowed. "Everything will be alright in the end." Emily tried to reassure him.

"Why didn't you tell me straight away?" He demanded.

"I didn't know how you would react. I didn't want to hurt you," they both stood there so overwhelmed, they didn't say a word.

"What happens now?" Katie murmured.

"I get better and life goes on."

"No matter what I'm always here…"

"So am I!" interrupted Katie.

The day finished and Emily and Katie said an emotional goodbye. Both aware that it could be the last time they spoke. Emily and Matt walked home. From outside they could hear Matt's parents arguing,

"Everything she does goes wrong she CANNOT stay here anymore. I knew I shouldn't have allowed it in the first place!"

"You can't do that to her… she's got nowhere else to go"

"She's got to go!"

"No, you can't! All the heartbreak that poor girl's gone through. You've seen how happy she makes him. I've never seen him smile as much as when he's with her!"

"She's cursed this family!"

"You can't just kick her out!" She grabbed his arm in desperation.

"Tough, she's going!" he pulls away and storms out of the room. Matt's mum hears footsteps going up the stairs and realises that her beloved son and Emily had heard every word. That evening there was an awkward silence. Emily and Matt sat apart on the sofa, while his parents sat in silence on separate chairs. Their TV was whispering the evening news of the day.

"And today, the weather has been stunning, over to the…"

Emily stood up and left the room. She grabbed a glass from the cupboard and placed it on the draining board behind the sink. Laying there, behind the tap was a large bread knife.

She had a sudden thought that she would end the household misery and free them from her. She filled up the glass with water, spilling some in the sink. She picked up the knife and firmly gripped it. She was shaking with fear. She didn't want to die, but thought it was best for everyone. She held the blade to her wrist. She could feel the cool steel against her skin. She relished the feeling. Just one small movement and it would all be over. No suffering. No cancer treatment. No more disappointment.

But the thought came to her – of the only person that made her feel happy. What it would do to him if he saw her laying on the floor. If he even cared, but he must care otherwise he wouldn't have been so kind to her. She hesitated. Barely keeping her hand still. There was a shadow behind her. She turned around and there was the one person who could stop her from making a mistake. She threw the knife into the sink and left the room.

Even though he was in the doorway, she managed to get through and get away. She ran up the stairs, into her room. He took her drink and carried it to her room. He knew what she was thinking. How she must feel.

His father had been so unkind to her. He had carried her drink to her room and placed it on the floor. She was sat on the floor, her body holding the door shut. He sat down on the other side of the door.

"Please, don't ever feel like you can't talk to me. I am here. I love you"

There was a silence and he stood up and walked away. She opened the door but didn't look at him. He saw in the reflection of the mirror that she was crying. Recently she had so much to cry about, not a day went past that she didn't. It tortured Matt to see her so upset every day. She didn't say a word to him that night. Embarrassed. Scared. Unable to speak.

When the next morning arrived, she was finally able to tell him what made her so upset and willing to die. After the argument with Matt's mum, his dad had spoken to Emily.

"He, he told me to leave. Get way away from here. Away from this house. From you." She said eventually.

"He… what?"

"Please don't get angry. We just need to forget this. All of it. Please I know you want to. I don't want all the stress. I just felt if I was gone, you could be a family again."

"We could never be a family without you."

CHAPTER TWO

The next few months passed. Emily had treatment for the cancer, and Matt's dad finally got over Emily being there. Things were still awkward, but not so bad. Every day, especially on treatment days, Matt was worried. So badly that he couldn't focus on schoolwork. Until one day Emily woke up feeling better than she had for months. Like herself again. Like a human again. She went to the doctors for her weekly check-up and they gave her the best news.

"From your results, I see no reason for you to return. We are satisfied that the cancer has gone."

Emily wanted to surprise him. So, she walked to school. She got there, just as the last bell of the day sounded. A herd of teenagers raced past her. Some pointed and whispered. Following behind was a solemn-looking Katie. She was deprived of her best friend.

Her face lit up like a small child's at Disneyland when she saw her. She ran up to her and hugged her. Emily's favourite teacher walked past.

"Oh, Emily. You're looking amazing. I've really missed you in my class. You need to come back and teach the others a thing or two."

The teacher walked away and behind was Matt. He was walking very slowly. He paid no attention to anything except the next step in front of him.

"Hey, babe." Emily said.

"What are you doing here, shouldn't you be at home?"

"Listen, I'm absolutely fine and the doctor said there is no reason to go back, so I can come back to school." Matt had a huge smile on his face the three of them had a group hug with so much happiness and large smiles. Nothing would spoil the happy moment.

Emily went back to school and even though she had been off school for so long; she was still a top student. Life couldn't get better for them. They were so happy and all back to normal. As close to normal as normal could get to them. They finished their GCSEs. Emily got all passes and Matt got some passes. They stood there on results' day, staring at their envelopes.

"I can't look... please open it." Emily said. They swapped envelopes and Matt opened hers. She stood there staring at him.

"What did I pass?"

"What didn't you pass?"

"What do you mean?" Matt turns the paper around. To their disbelief she had passes every subject.

That day she visited her dad's grave.

"I did it dad. I can't believe it. I've actually done it."

Matt appeared and put his hand on her shoulder. "He would be so proud of you... I am."

CHAPTER THREE

The next few years passed. Emily and Matt were still so happy together. They bought a house together. Small, but perfect. Emily was a very successful singer and Matt had a songwriter job. Emily had been working very hard, so Matt wanted to surprise her with a once in a lifetime holiday. After everything she went through, she sure deserved it. Her dad promised her a trip to every Disneyland in the world, but when he died that promise had died to. She came home from work and Matt had a special evening planned.

He had attempted to cook her dinner, but he wasn't very good.

"Hello," came a voice from the door. Matt came rushing out of the kitchen covering the door to the surprise. She went upstairs to change clothes and peaked in the door. She saw the table decorated in flowers and candles.

"Can I come down now?"

"Umm… yeah," she came downstairs to be greeted by fancy decorations. Matt pulled out a chair and she sat down. She took a sip of the wine in front of her.

"Can I smell burning?" she said. Matt bolted into the kitchen where the food he had spent hours making was a black mess. He looked very sad. She stood up and looked at the mess of her kitchen.

"There's a fish and chip shop around the corner." She said barely managing the words without laughing. She left the house and came back with an arm full of food. Matt took it off her and started plating it up. She sat down and Matt handed her a tray. They sat and talked about everything that happened that day and once they had finished Matt removed the tray revealing a large envelope.

"What's this?" she asked.

"Open it" she opened it revealing plane tickets to Paris dated the following week.

"What's this?" she asked again.

"Tickets for you and me, to Paris."

"Are you serious? This is amazing."

"And LA and Florida and China and Japan. It is 12 weeks long."

"What?"

"Every Disney in the world and other stuff of course."

"Oh my god! I can't believe it."

"It's been so hard keeping from you. And everything's sorted you don't need to worry about anything." She stood up and gave him the biggest hug she could.

The day of the first flight arrived, and Matt's friend Adam picked them up to take them to the airport. They both got in the car and they were about to leave when Emily shouted, "Wait. I forgot something." She got out of the car and went back into the house. Meanwhile, Matt was in the car. "Do you think she will say yes?" he was holding a little velvet covered box.

"Are you joking?" Adam asked.

"Of course, she will. Why are you doubting that?"

"I don't know. I just love her so much I can't imagine how I would feel if she didn't."

Suddenly, the car door opened, and Matt thrust the box into his pocket.

"Right I'm ready. Let's go to Disney!"

The car drove off and they travelled to the airport and then to France. They arrived in Paris in the evening and Matt booked a fancy restaurant overlooking the Eiffel Tower. It was dark and all the lights were turned on. She got dressed in the nicest thing she had, and they walked to the restaurant.

They sat outside facing the Eiffel Tower. The waiter came and asked them what they wanted, and she ordered something she couldn't even pronounce. To her surprise the waiter brought back a plate of fancy presented fish and chips.

"You look gorgeous by the way." Matt said.

"Not so bad yourself."

They were both astonished with the view. Matt dropped his fork onto the floor. Emily turned around.

"I can't take you anywhere, can I?" she continued to look at the view. She was in paradise. Meanwhile, Matt had one leg and one foot against the ground. He was holding out his hands with a small open box. It held a silver ring with a dazzling diamond. She turned around to see him. She looked so shocked. Speechless.

"As a very wise grandma once said: everything happens for a reason, and that's why I met you. So, will you make me the happiest man alive, even though I can't be much happier?"

It was Emily's grandma who always said, "Everything happens for a reason".

Emily was so shocked by his sudden gesture that she didn't say anything. Matt started looking worried because she didn't say yes.

"Oh, my! Yes. Yes! Of course."

"You will?" he stood up, disorientated. He couldn't believe she said yes.

"Are you kidding? Of course. Oh my god. I love you." He took the ring from the box and put it on her finger. He leaned over the table and hugged her. They finished their meal, went back to their room, and their holiday begun.

They woke up and went to Disneyland. Later that week they went out for dinner and Emily had an unusually big appetite. She ate so much. The next day she was sick. But it only lasted the morning, and by lunch time she was fine. That happened every day for the whole holiday. She thought there was something wrong, so she secretly went to the pharmacy.

She described her symptoms and they told her something shocking. She was handed a pregnancy test. She went straight to the toilet and the result was even more surprising. It was positive. She threw it into the bin. Later that day Matt went into the bathroom and found the test.

"Emily, what is this?"

"What's what?" he held up the test.

"It's not mine. Where did you find it?"

"On the floor."

"It must have been there before we got here. It's not mine." He put it down and they carried on with the day. But once he walked away and was out of view, he was really disappointed. He wanted a baby more than anything.

Weeks passed and they had the best time of their life. Weeks that they will never forget for the rest of their life. However long it would last. They spent their last day before flying home at the pool.

One more perfect, relaxing day before returning to reality. They were sunbathing, enjoying the peace.

"I'm getting in," she said, taking off her top and stretching.

It had been eleven weeks since she found out she was pregnant, and her stomach was slightly bigger and rounded.

"No offence babe, but you, um you…" he pointed to her stomach. She instantly covered it and got into the pool.

"I told you: I have eaten too much on this holiday." She pulled a weird looking face at him and glided into the water. He stood up, ran, and jumped into the pool like a child, making a huge splash. Emily thought of the baby and how she didn't know how to tell him. She was scared that Matt wouldn't want her.

"Are you okay?" he said as he put his arm around her and pulled her closer.

"Perfect." She said after a pause.

"I want to get married." He said.

"We are."

"No, I mean tomorrow. I can't wait for you to be my wife. Mine forever. When we get home tomorrow, we should get married."

"Really?"

"Of course."

"Okay then, tomorrow." They enjoyed their last evening before flying back home.

That evening they got dressed and went to the registry office. It was just Emily, Matt and Katie who went. But it was enough. They stood there with cheap bouquets of flowers. Emily and Matt stood there facing each other. Matt pulled out this piece of paper and started reading. Now it was her turn. She held his hand and subtlety placed them on her stomach.

"I love you so much and you have saved my life and given me something I could not have even wished for and I will never forget that. Now it's just you and me and…"

"And what?" he stood there silent and confused. After a very long pause he realised.

"Are you? Are you pregnant?" she said nothing just nodded her head. His face lit up like a child at Christmas.

"Are you pleased?" she asked apprehensively.

"Pleased? This is the best new ever. I love you so much."

"It's me, and you, and Baby against the world."

CHAPTER FOUR

They spent weeks in Heaven. Nothing could spoil their life now. Matt worked harder and was earning lots more money and becoming very successful. Emily stayed at home and decorated the baby's room, but she didn't tell Matt about it. It was the day of the scan and they desperately wanted to know the gender. She wanted a boy and he wanted a girl. The room had white walls and one light in the corner to make the screen brighter. They nervously sat down and waited. The nurse came in and checked on the baby.

"Do you want to know the gender?"

"Yes please" they both said.

"It's a… boy!"

Their faces both lit up. This was one of the best days of their life.

"Do you have a name in mind?" Matt asked.

"Yes, Archie after my dad. You don't mind, do you?" she looked at him.

"It's perfect." She started to get teary, looked up at the ceiling and held her stomach firmly but not too hard.

"Look Dad, it's a boy. A grandson. Just like you always wanted."

"I'm sure he's very proud of you," said the nurse.

Months passed and she finished the room and it was beautiful. It had pastel coloured walls and lots of furniture. It had a giant yellow "A" on the front of the door and Matt never suspected anything. Archie was nearly due. A couple of weeks from his arrival.

Everything was perfect. Just perfect. But she was about to discover something that would significantly change their lives. After a long day of finishing the room, she had a long bath. She sat there for a while and when she looked down, she found a lump on her leg. She got dressed and went to the hospital as quickly as possible.

"I'm afraid to tell you that the cancer has come back and…"

"And…"

"I don't know how long you've got left."

"What? I'm dying? How long would you say?" there was a pause.

"How long!"

"This is just statistics everyone is different."

"How long!"

"Could be weeks,"

"What?! Weeks?" The nurse looked like she was hiding something.

"What else?"

"Could be days…"

"Days?! Oh, my god. At least tell me my baby will be born and I'll make it to see Christmas? At least he'll be born?"

"We are unable to tell."

"Are you serious I might die and take him with me?"

"Unfortunately, it's possible."

She stormed out. Once out of sight, she cried. Cried and cried. How could she tell him? She went home and waited for him to come home.

Hours later, he came home. Emily was worried sick.

"Hello?" he said peeking through the door.

"Matt, I have something to tell you." He didn't hear her.

"At work there was this woman and she…"

"Matt please. It's important."

"She asked me…"

"Matthew!" she never called him that. Ever. So, he knew it was serious.

"What?"

"I went to the doctors because I found this." She pointed at her leg where she found it. Matt looked very worried.

"And she said that I have not long left to live could be weeks. Could be days." She started to look very pale and ill. She lost her balance and almost fell over. Matt put his arms out to catch her and she fell. He caught her. He struggled to get his phone out of his trouser pocket while holding her.

"Ambulance please. Emily, babe please wake up. Open your eyes. Come on please. Look at me, look at me." The ambulance came and took her to the hospital.

She had her own room in the intensive care unit. She was dying. She would take Archie with her to. The hospital examined her, but she was too ill to undergo an emergency caesarean. It was too much of a risk. It was inevitable they both were going to die.

Matt went and got a coffee and when he returned, he looked into the window and saw a nurse adjusting her pillow. She gave Emily a drink and walked out of the room. She just sat there and starred at the white wall. When she turned around, she saw him looking at her. Whenever they saw each other from a distance they would make a heart with their hands. So, when he saw her, he did it. She smiled and copied him. He walked in and sat down.

"Hey, you okay?" he said. He held her hand tightly.

"Not really."

"It's okay. You're going to be okay."

"No, I'm not. I'm dying. We know that. I've let you down. I'm so sorry." She covered her stomach.

"What are you sorry for?"

"You're not getting a son and I've ruined your life; made it a misery. And I'm so sorry. But I want you to move on. Find someone to give you lots of gorgeous children. Everything I couldn't. Everything happens for a reason, so the universe is telling you to move on. Earn lots of money. Live a better life without me."

"How can life be good without you?"

"I gave you hope and tore it away from you. I can't apologise enough. You have made me feel so happy. I love you so much." Her eyes started to shut.

She tried to move her hand out of his, but he held it tighter. Her eyes shut completely. He put his hand on her stomach. Suddenly the life support machine beeped.

"No. No… look at me. You can't leave me. You can't. Please, please look at me." The machine didn't stop. Ongoing beeping echoed. Two nurses rushed in. Everything happened in slow motion and everything was a blur. One nurse was working with the equipment and the other was dragging Matt out of the room. He tried to resist but she wouldn't let him. He managed to touch her stomach one last time.

He stood outside and looked through the window, but the nurse had closed it. Where she was in a rush, she didn't close it properly and at an angle he could see through. After a minute the nurses stopped and looked at each other. They paused. Then pulled up a blank white sheet over her. She was gone. The nurses locked him out, but he tried to open it. He desperately tried to pull open the door. He pulled and pulled but didn't get it open. He fell to his knees. Not strong enough to stand and he cried. Cried and cried. He lost the one he loves and his child in minutes. He had to go home. Alone.

When he arrived home, he came to find an amazing surprise. He went upstairs and accidently went into the wrong room he found the spare storage room filled and decorated with baby things. He was so shocked that she could do it all on her own and he didn't realise. He spent his days alone, sleeping on her side of the bed and not eating properly. The news of her death spread, and everybody knew.

It was the day of the funeral. He worked so hard to try to get it just right. He walked down the road to the nearest church. He was amazed by the amount of people there and looking sad. He thought he went to the wrong church. He never knew she was so popular. He went inside and sat down. There were lots of people who apologised and gave him their sympathy. He didn't even know them. Then Katie walked in. She looked lost. She walked up to Matt. He stood up and gave her a hug. They sat next to each other. Then Adam walked in. He sat next to them too. Matt had a flashback.

He remembered when she told him about the times she went to a funeral, but by herself. Matt felt lonely without her but couldn't imagine how she felt. The vicar spoke but it didn't matter. He just couldn't believe she had gone, and he would never see her again. The funeral was a blur. He was stuck in a constant state of numbness. She was gone so why did anything else matter? No matter what was said about her it didn't sink in. it didn't matter. Nothing mattered. Nothing could bring her back. He was frozen. Everything happened in slow motion. Until it was his turn to speak. He slowly shuffled to the front of the church. He spoke about how good she was. How kind she was. He didn't believe a word of it. It didn't matter how amazing she was, he couldn't think of anything to say. Nothing mattered anymore.

Later, at the wake, Matt stood alone. Looking out at the garden but not really seeing it.

"Hello, are you okay. I heard. And I'm so sorry." Adam put his hand on Matt. He hit his hand off him. "She didn't deserve it. I thought we could go out for a drink tonight. I haven't seen you in ages." He sat up from the bed.

"Get out. How dare you. Get out." Adam didn't move. Matt stood up, got close to his face. "I'm not going out and being your wing man while you find another one-night stand, for you to just forget about by the morning."

"Mate, that's not fair."

"You know it's true."

Adam turned around and stormed out of the house. Matt ran into Archie's room for comfort. It didn't work. Adam's words made him so furious and made the grief really unbearable. He got angrier and angrier by his words until he set the anger free. He screams and his fist flies through the air, knocking a large picture frame from the wall. It hits the ground and smashes. Emily had covered a large part of the wall and had created a collage of their favourite pictures. A picture from every amazing memory they had.

Matt realised what he had done, so he bent down and picked up a large piece of glass. It pierces his skin and he starts to bleed. He runs down the stairs to cover his injured hand. He picks up a random cloth in the draw and covers the wound. He looks out of the window. On the windowsill there is an envelope.

He picks it up and opens it and reads it. It is a letter from Emily saying her goodbyes. She decorated the envelope and made it look as presentable as possible. However, there were two drops of water on it and the ink beneath made it hard to read. Matt realised something at that point. He realises he cannot live without her and if he did it would be a misery. He couldn't escape her. He didn't want to escape her. He read the letter. His one final memory and possession that linked him to his wife.

My Dearest Love,

I know it's my time to leave and I cannot apologise enough for the trauma I put you through. I hate what I have done to you. I just want to say thank you for making my life so amazing. I couldn't imagine it without you, and for that I will be forever grateful. Every second with you has been incredible and you could never understand how much I love you. I'm so sorry I cannot give you what you want so promise me you will find a better girl that could make your true wishes come true because I couldn't. It hurts me to think you are not getting what you deserve. Promise me. Please. So now it's time to say goodbye. I hope you find this letter. Just remember I love you. Always.

Em xx

He goes back upstairs, back in Archie's room. He clears up the smashed glass. He finds a large jagged piece with a sharp point. He puts it in his pocket with the letter and one of his favourite photos from the frame. Then he slowly walks through all of the rooms in the house. Once he's finished he walks to Emily's grave.

"I've found your letter. How can you say just move on? I love you so much and I am struggling on my own." He removes the letter and the piece of glass from his pockets. The photograph fell out of his pocket and blew away in the wind. He barely notices. He is too focused on what he was about to do.

"I can't live without you. I love you." He stares at the glass and settles it on his wrist. It gives him a flashback of when Emily wanted to kill herself, only she was too scared. Matt is not. He knew what he wanted to do. He looked at the glass, the letter, and her grave. His hand slowly moved across his wrist. He took a deep breath. Then he did it. He fell to the floor.

Now he was dead too.

Later that day Matt's parents visited her grave. They went to their house and there was no answer. So they assumed he would be with her. They walked and saw him lying still on the grass. She thought he was asleep. She walked over to him, kneeled on the ground.

"Hey, wake up."

There was no reply.

"Come on, its two o'clock. You need to…" she lifted her hand and there was blood. She realised he wasn't sleeping. She screamed and her husband came rushing over. He fell to the ground in shock. They were just staring at their son. They knew he was dead. His dad got up and walked away.

"At least he was happy." His mum said.

"What do you mean happy? He killed himself."

"He had a good life with her."

"Our son is dead. I knew I shouldn't have let you bring that girl in. She brought a curse to our family. How could this be a good thing?"

"We couldn't make him happy and she could. You saw how happy he was with her. She needed us. How could you just leave her in that situation? She didn't deserve it. If you could just leave her like that then you are a horrible person."

He walked away leaving her by her dead son and Emily's fresh grave, who had been like a daughter to her. Now she had no-one.

The story ends when true love gets in the way of an ordinary family. They were destined to be together forever to meet and fall in love.

Well, after all, everything happens for a reason.

JESSICA STEVENS

EVERYTHING HAPPENS FOR A REASON

ABOUT THE AUTHOR

Jessica Stevens is a 15 year old Secondary school student. The idea for *Everything Happens* came to her randomly one day. Jessica originally had no intention to write a book. However the idea would not go away and when she was offered the chance to write a book, she took it with both hands.

ABOUT THE PUBLISHER

Spencer Press is an imprint of Upbury Press
Publishers, dedicated to publishing quality
books containing a strong female lead.
Upbury Press is a proud and modest company
with its offices near London in the United
Kingdom.

JESSICA STEVENS

JESSICA STEVENS

Printed in Great Britain
by Amazon